G g

# Grandma, Grandpa, and the Letter G

*Alphabet Friends*

*by Cynthia Klingel and Robert B. Noyed*

The Child's World

**The Child's World**

Published in the United States of America
by The Child's World®
P.O. Box 326
Chanhassen, MN 55317-0326
800-599-READ
www.childsworld.com

The Child's World®: Mary Berendes, Publishing Director

Editorial Directions, Inc.: E. Russell Primm, Editorial
Director; Emily Dolbear, Line Editor; Ruth Martin,
Editorial Assistant; Linda S. Koutris, Photo Researcher
and Selector

Photographs ©: Corbis: Cover & 11; Bohemian Nomad
Picturemakers/Corbis: 12; Bruce Smith/Fratelli Studio/
Corbis: 15; George D. Lepp/Corbis: 16; Richard
Hamilton Smith/Corbis: 19; Ryan McVay/Photodisc/
Picture Quest: 20.

**Library of Congress Cataloging-in-Publication Data**
Klingel, Cynthia Fitterer.
  Grandma, Grandpa, and the letter G / by Cynthia
Klingel and Robert B. Noyed.
    p. cm. — (Alphabet readers)
Summary: A simple story about a young girl's summer
visit to with her grandparents introduces the letter "g".
  ISBN 1-59296-097-9 (alk. paper)
  [1. Grandparents—Fiction. 2. Alphabet.] I. Noyed,
Robert B. II. Title. III. Series.
  PZ7.K6798Gr 2003
  [E]—dc21                                    2003006532

**Note to parents and educators:**

The first skill children acquire before becoming successful readers is individual letter recognition. The Alphabet Friends series has been created with the needs of young learners in mind. Each engaging book begins by showing the difference between the capital letter and the lowercase letter. In each of the books on the vowels and the consonants c and g, children are introduced to the different sounds that the letter can make. Finally, children see that the letters can be found at the beginning of a word, in the middle of a word, and in most cases, at the end of a word.

Following the introduction, children meet their Alphabet Friends. The friend in each story encounters many words that include the featured letter of that book. Each noun that begins with the title letter is highlighted in red with the initial letter of the word in bold. Above the word is a rebus drawing that establishes a strong picture cue.

At the end of each book, we have included three words lists. Can your young learners find all the words in each book with the title letter in them?

Let's learn about the letter **G.**

The letter **G** can look like this: **G.**

The letter **G** can also look like this: **g.**

The letter **g** makes two different sounds.

One sound is the hard sound,

like in the word girl.

**g**irl

The other sound is the soft sound,

like in the word giraffe.

giraffe

The letter **g** can be at the
beginning of a word, like golf.

**g**olf

The letter **g** can be in the
middle of a word, like eagle.

ea**g**le

The letter **g** can be at the

end of a word, like dog.

do**g**

My name is **G**race. I had a good

summer. I got to do many great things.

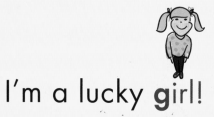

I'm a lucky **g**irl!

I stayed at my grandparents' house.

Grandma was glad I got to come.

Grandpa George played golf with me.

My golf ball got lost in the grass.

I helped **G**randpa mow the **g**rass.

I saw a **g**opher hiding in the **g**rass.

It made me giggle to see the **g**opher

run away.

I got to go to the zoo. I saw a **g**iraffe

and a **g**rizzly bear. I growled at the

**g**rizzly bear.

I had a great summer with **G**randma

and **G**randpa. Now I am ready to go

to first **g**rade!

# Fun Facts

The **g**iraffe is the tallest animal in the world. Male **g**iraffes are often more than 17 feet (5.3 meters) tall. **G**iraffes are so tall because of their long legs and necks. Their legs are 6 feet (1.8 m) long and their necks are often longer. Yet a **g**iraffe has only seven neck bones—the same amount that a human has!

**G**ophers are small, furry animals that live underground. **G**ophers dig tunnels with their front teeth and the claws on their front feet. We use our hands to touch, but **g**ophers can use their tails. When **g**ophers back up in the tunnels, their tails help them to feel their way around.

**G**rizzly bears are a kind of brown bear. They are large and powerful. Adult **g**rizzly bears can grow to be 8 feet (2.4 m) tall. Sometimes **g**rizzly bears eat as much as 90 pounds (40 kg) of food a day! **G**rizzly bears live in the western United States and Canada.

# To Read More

## About the Letter G
Ballard, Peg. *Gifts for Gus: The Sound of G.* Chanhassen, Minn.: The Child's World, 2000.

## About Giraffes
Crozat, Francois. *I Am a Little Giraffe.* New York: Barron's Educational Series, 1995.
Kennaway, Adrienne. *Baby Giraffe.* Long Island City, N.Y.: Star Bright Books, 1999.
Markert, Jenny. *Giraffes.* Chanhassen, Minn.: The Child's World, 2001.

## About Gophers
Johnston, Tony, and Trip Park (illustrator). *Gopher up Your Sleeve.* Flagstaff, Ariz.: Rising Moon, 2001.
Sargent, Dave, Pat Sargent, and Blaine Sapaugh (illustrator). *Tunnel King.* Prairie Grove, Ark.: Ozark Publishing, 1996.

## About Grizzly Bears
Manfried, Lucia, and Lynne Cherry. *Grizzly Bear.* New York: Dutton, 1987.
McDonald, Mary Ann. *Grizzlies.* Chanhassen, Minn.: The Child's World, 1997.
Senshu, Noriko. *Sonny's Dream.* Charlottesville, Va.: Hampton Roads, 2000.

# Words with G

### Words with G at the Beginning

George
giggle
giraffe
girl
glad
go
golf
golf ball
good
gopher
got
Grace
grade
grandma
grandpa
grandparents
grass
great
grizzly bear
growled

### Words with G in the Middle

beginning
eagle
giggle
things

### Words with G at the End

beginning
dog
hiding

### About the Authors

*Cynthia Klingel has worked as a high school English teacher and an elementary teacher. She is currently the curriculum director for a Minnesota school district. Cynthia Klingel lives with her family in Mankato, Minnesota.*

*Robert B. Noyed started his career as a newspaper reporter. Since then, he has worked in communications and public relations for a Minnesota school district for more than fourteen years. Robert B. Noyed lives with his family in Brooklyn Center, Minnesota.*